# Colors

# Sylvia Carlton

ROYSTON
Publishing

BK Royston Publishing
P. O. Box 4321
Jeffersonville, IN  47131
502-802-5385
http://www.bkroystonpublishing.com
bkroystonpublishing@gmail.com

© Copyright – 2020

Cover Design:  Gad Elite Cover Designs

ISBN:  978-1-951941-76-5

Printed in the United States of America

# Other Books by this Author

Inspiration – Copyright March 2020

# DEDICATION

This writing is dedicated to my niece, *Cynthia Langston.*

Simply put, I promised her that I would place her name front and center in my second book (private conversation — don't ask). More than that, I am thrilled to do so, because she is my first niece. There can only be one "First" of anything. First child, first grandchild, first day of school, first home, first car. You get the idea.

Yes, Cynthia is my first niece and the little sister that I never had. My mother loved to refer to her as "My Ollllldest Grandchild." And yes, she would drag out the word "Oldest" for a full five seconds.

At any rate, while I have 22 nieces and nephews, Cynthia is and will always be, the first. That can never change. Thus, this dedication.

Thank you, Cynthia, for making me a proud Auntie.

.

## SO. . .

First and foremost, let me say welcome. If you are reading this, then thank you so much for your support. I am thrilled that you have decided to join me on this adventure. I call it an "adventure" because that is exactly what it is, and I think you will agree with me by the time you finish the final chapter.

Now let's turn our attention to the characters that you are about to meet here. They have been waiting for some time to make your acquaintance and I think you will enjoy meeting them, as well. Some people are unforgettable from the moment you meet them. Others, not so much. The new friends that you are about to make here are all equally memorable. They all have their own distinct "colorful" (pun intended) personalities.

FULL DISCLOSURE: Even though I am the author and supposedly in charge here, we all know there are always some family members who just insist on having things their way. I am referring specifically to Red, a one-of-a-kind diva. She makes a grand entrance wherever she goes, and you never have to wonder what she is thinking. She will let it be known. Anyway, I won't give away too much; I will let her speak for herself — and that she does very well.

A round of thanks is in order for the many people in my life without whom I would not be who I am today. My parents, Sim and Hallie Carlton, were the driving force behind all of my achievements. In any of my writings, I will always make some mention of my parents, aunts, uncles, and siblings who all had an integral part in my upbringing. My late Aunt Ella was such a jewel and one of the kindest people you ever met. My late Aunt Gussie always kept it real and loved and lived life to the fullest. My late Uncle J.B. was a great disciplinarian but loved us to no end. My late Uncle Tubbie was someone who I could always go to for advice and wise counsel. Last but certainly not least, my Aunt Ann keeps us all in check and does it with so much love.

I am thankful for being raised with brothers and sisters whom I learned from and who helped shape my life. I hold dear to my heart the memory of my oldest sister, Betty. If she could only see me now, I believe she would be proud. Even though we are separated by many miles, my sister Katie and I share a special bond, and can communicate via technology. What a great thing e-mail has turned out to be! I can't say enough about my sister Colie, who has the biggest heart and is always willing to listen and advise. I applaud my sister Doris, who has been my partner in crime many times over and always encourages me. My brothers, Simmie and Curtis, have both been excellent examples of what a real man should look like. I would not be me without all of you.

Special Mention -- thanks to my proofreader and sister, Doris, for the wonderful cover design idea.

Lastly, if you did not read my previous publication, "Inspiration," I encourage you to go over to Amazon and pick up a copy. Or you can contact me, and I am sure I can scrounge up a copy to sign and get it out to you. It is in no way a precursor to this book; on the contrary, it is at the other end of the spectrum when compared to "Colors" but it will show you a side of my writing that I guarantee you will enjoy. It contains things that make you go "hmmmm...." It is thought-provoking, a bit humorous in parts, and a short but powerful read.

So now, without further ado, let's go and meet the stars of the show, who have been anxiously waiting in the wings.

# CHAPTER ONE

Angela sat in her physics class listening to the instructor drone on about light and energy and electricity. It was such a beautiful day, and she was finding it hard to concentrate. She couldn't care less at this point about how matter and energy related. The subject of matter just didn't matter, and she had no energy. The clock seemed to be moving in slow motion. It was the first week of May, and graduation would be in just three short weeks. Where had the time gone? It seemed only yesterday that she and her twin brother, Aaron, had entered high school. The vibration of Angela's cell phone brought her out of her reverie. She glanced down and saw that it was a text from her father that said, "please call home." Angela thought that was strange; what was it that couldn't wait until she got home? Maybe he wanted her to stop and pick up something on her way in. She was sure that was it. She tried to dismiss it, but yet she had an uneasy feeling, much like the sixth sense that one has when something just is not right. Finally, after eternity and a day, the bell rang signaling the end of class. "Thank God," Angela said out loud. It had been a long day. Little did she know that it was about to be an even longer night. She quickly gathered her things and headed for her locker. She met

Aaron in the hallway just as he was leaving his class two doors down.

"Aaron," she said, frowning, "I got a text from Dad saying to call home. What do you suppose that's about?"

"Beats me," Aaron chuckled as he shoved his backpack in his locker. Aaron never brought books home and seldom studied, but somehow managed to get straight A's in all his classes. He often teased Angela that he was the twin with the brains, and she was the one with the beauty. Just then, his cell phone beeped. It was the same text from their father — "please call home." Angela's palms began to sweat as she dialed her home number.

"Dad, it's Angie. We got your message to call home. What's going on?" Instinctively she asked, "Is there something wrong with Mom?" Their mother was a partner at the firm of Douglas and Bates, one of the most prestigious firms in San Antonio, and had spent the week in Houston working on trial preparation. She could hear the apprehension in her father's voice as he spoke slowly.

"Angie, I sent you and Aaron a text because I didn't want you to hear any news before you got home."

"News? What kind of news?" Angela's voice caught in her throat and her phone started to slip from her hand.

Aaron took the phone. "Dad, what's going on?"

His father chose his words carefully. "Mom was flying in from Houston this afternoon and the plane went down. Some of the passengers survived, but not all of them. They haven't released any names yet. We need to head over to the airport."

Angela had always enjoyed going to the airport. As a child, her dad used to take her and Aaron to watch the planes arriving and departing. It was a small but simple pleasure, and they never tired of watching the huge planes, which looked like gigantic birds. They would watch the planes and pretend that they were about to board them to travel to faraway places. Angie would say something like "That's my plane and I will be flying out to Europe." Aaron would reply with "Well, my plane is bigger than yours and my crew will be taking me to Africa for a week."

Their family was small, but close-knit. Twins ran in the family. Her maternal grandmother had an identical twin sister. As Angela and Aaron entered the airport, they held hands tightly, sharing a bond that only twins share, silently communicating as only twins do, and praying that they had not been dealt the card that they feared they had. This time the airport held no joy for them. For the first time, Angie dreaded walking through the doors that as a child she had raced through, looking forward to an afternoon of imagination and fun.

James Burke was a tall, muscular man. He had always been health-conscious, and he and his wife enjoyed cooking healthy meals and working out at the gym as often as they could. But on this day, James looked small and drawn. Since he had gotten the news earlier about the plane crash, his whole world had stopped. His eyes were glazed and staring, almost as if he were unable to focus, much as a blind person does. Angie felt helpless looking at her father and found herself hoping for his sake that this was all just a horrific mistake. But as she held tightly to her twin's hand, she knew that the worst kind of reality was unfolding. As they got closer to the information desk, everything seemed to be moving in slow motion, probably because she wanted it to. The longer it took to reach the desk, the more they could put off hearing the words that would possibly confirm their worst fears.

* * *

Have you ever associated people with colors? If James Burke was a color, he would be Purple — strong, stoic, royal. But on this day, he was more gray than anything else. Still, dull and almost lifeless. After 25 years of marriage, a great career and two wonderful children, James was now facing the unimaginable. At this point, nothing else mattered. Not the careers, not the promotions, not the expansive home with the lavish furnishings. All that mattered was his beloved Pamela. Pamela — the love of his life, the apple of his eye, his best friend.

Pamela Burke would be the color Blue. A very calm blue, like the sky on a perfect summer day. She was a peaceful person, the kind of person who could diffuse even the most traumatic of situations. She always kept a level head and had the ability to make everyone around her feel at ease. She was a no-nonsense attorney, tough as nails in the courtroom, but the perfect wife and mother at home. She struck the ideal balance between family and career. Soft, sky-blue Pamela. But now a thunderstorm had come and washed away the beautiful blue hues.

Aaron would be the color Green. The color of life, always energized, well-liked by his peers, and an all-around athlete who made school and studying seem effortless. But as he walked into the airport, Aaron resembled an exceedingly small child, apprehensive about approaching what was ahead of him.

"We're here to inquire about the people that were involved in the plane that went down," Aaron said in a voice that didn't even sound like his own. The woman at the desk pointed in the direction of a room at the end of the hallway.

"Right that way, sir."

"Thank you," Aaron said, again in the strange voice, and led the way down the hall.

"In the Pink" is a phrase that means feeling good and doing

well. That was Angie to a tee. Bright, Pink Angie, always feeling great and forever optimistic. But on this day, a day that had turned black for the Burke family, pink was nowhere to be found. Angie's head felt like it was a bowling ball sitting on top of a marshmallow. Tears streamed down her face as reality started to set in. She willed herself to remain calm, praying and hoping for the best.

They were ushered into a room with friends and family members of all the passengers on the plane. It was strangely quiet. Some people were silently praying, others were crying. A woman who was obviously a volunteer was sitting at the back of the room at a small table that had fresh brewed coffee, water and snacks. Angie found herself wondering why do all volunteers look alike? It was as if they were ordered from Amazon and brought in for situations like this. They always had a very calm demeanor and managed to keep their composure no matter what.

Just then, an airport employee entered the room. In his hand he held a flight manifest. One by one, he started to announce the names of all confirmed passengers who were on board the plane, and which hospital they had been taken to. There were two hospitals that were attending to the victims, and

the passengers with the most
severe injuries were taken to the
hospital with the more
sophisticated trauma center. He
did not, however, disclose who
had survived and who had not.
Pamela Burke had been taken to
Bayside Medical, so James and the
twins headed for the hospital.

# CHAPTER TWO

Kenny was counting down the last five minutes on his stationary bike. He tried to get in at least thirty minutes every day. If it was not too hot outside, he also jogged for another twenty minutes. He lived with his mother, Debra Roberts, in a small house about half a mile from San Antonio South Academy, where he was a senior. He had applied and been accepted to several out-of-state colleges, but right after Christmas his father had dropped a bomb and asked his mother for a divorce. Kenny was devastated; he never saw it coming. His mother had told him afterward that they had been having marital problems for some time, but they had kept it hidden from Kenny. After receiving this news, Kenny had decided to attend a local community college for his first two years because he did not want to leave his mother alone. He had continued to receive acceptance letters — "Dear Mr. Roberts, we are pleased to inform you…." He didn't even open them anymore and made sure that his mother did not see them in the mail. She tried to convince him to go away to college, but he had made up his mind that he would stay home with her. He was an only child, and had no problem admitting that he was a mama's boy. He and his father had always been close, but now he was starting to resent him for what he had done. After his father left the home, Kenny's mother had gone into a state of depression. Even though she knew the separation was imminent, it had affected her more than she had anticipated. She went to work each day, came home and stared at the television for a couple of hours, and went to bed. She rarely ate dinner, saying that she had eaten a big lunch. Kenny knew that wasn't true, but all he could do was pray that she would get through it. He knew it would take time, but he hoped that it would be sooner rather than later.

You never know how something can affect you, until it actually happens. You can watch other people go through life-changing experiences, but you can't truly understand how it feels

until it comes to your door. Kenny
tried to get her to see a doctor, but
she refused. She worked as a
counselor at a shelter for battered
women. She was exceptionally
good at what she did and always
knew the right words to say to the
women whose lives were in
disarray. Now, it was she who
needed counseling. What's the
phrase…physician heal thyself?
Debra was normally yellow —
bright and cheery, always smiling
and upbeat. She had the perfect
personality to work with battered
women. She made them feel
hopeful despite their
circumstances. But Kenny had to
push all that aside for now,
because graduation was right
around the corner and prom was in
one week. He was struggling with

the thought of talking to his girlfriend, Angie, about their relationship. They had been growing apart, for no specific reason; somehow the attraction was just not there anymore. They had decided to go ahead and attend the prom together out of respect for each other, but then end their relationship altogether. In January, a transfer student by the name of Julie had come to San Antonio South. Kenny was attracted to her at first sight, and eventually she took up more of his time and attention than Angie.

"Kenny, Kenny, are you there?" Julie burst through the door, her ponytail bouncing up and down as she practically skipped across the room. "Hey there, Marathon Man!" She gave Kenny a kiss on the cheek and plopped down on the couch next to his bike. "Almost done?"

"Yes, about three minutes to go" Kenny smiled back. Julie's color would be orange, one of the brightest colors in the rainbow. She was bright and bouncy and lit up any room. She was the perfect complement for Kenny, who was teal. He was calm and collected, never bright or flashy, just a cool teal. Opposites attract. Kenny looked over at Julie, who had taken out her cell phone and was checking Facebook while she waited for him to finish. He remembered how she had walked into his history class on her first day at San Antonio South, and he couldn't take his eyes off of her. There was just something about her.

Julie had seen Kenny and Angie around the school and knew they were a couple, but she also knew that Kenny was attracted to her. But she did not dare cross the line, even though they both knew there was something there. Finally, it had been Kenny who had approached Julie first and asked her out. She accepted, and they went out that weekend and Kenny told her about his and Angie's relationship, and that they were attending prom as a mutual gesture of friendship, but calling it quits after that.

Kenny got off the bike and was doing some stretches when

his phone rang. He looked over and saw that it was Angie. "It's Angie," he looked over at Julie. Julie made a clown face and said, "Go ahead and answer. I promise to be quiet."

Kenny laughed as he picked up the call. "Hey Angie, what's up?" He listened for a minute and then said, "Oh my God, I will be right there!" Julie saw the look of horror on Kenny's face.

"What is it, Kenny? What's wrong?"

"Angie is at the hospital. Mrs. Burke was in a plane crash."

"I'm going with you." Julie sprang off the couch.

"I don't think that would be a good idea." Kenny frowned.

"Yes, I think it would be," Julie countered. "Listen, Kenny, Angie already knows about us, and this is not about us at this point. Of course, this is horrible, but right now both of you need my support. Let's go."

When Kenny and Julie arrived at the hospital, she told him to go ahead in and she would park the car. After all, he was closer to the family than she was. Kenny was directed to the family/surgical waiting room. James Burke and Aaron were sitting on the far side of the room. Kenny rushed over to where they were sitting. "Mr. Burke, I'm so sorry. Has there been any news yet?" James Burke looked as if he had been run over by a cement truck. He stared blankly at Kenny and finally managed to utter, "Nothing yet. We do know that she survived, but we don't know the extent of her injuries."

Just as Kenny was about to ask where Angie was, she walked into the room. She had gone out to get some air. "Angie," Kenny hugged her, "We will get through this."

Angie's eyes filled with tears. She was crying for her mom, for her brother and her father. She was crying because she would have given anything to make things between her and Kenny go back to the way they once were. She wished for a magic bullet to turn things around. She wished she could turn back the hands of time and have the power not to let this day have ever happened.

The entire weight of the world seemed to be resting on Angie's shoulders. Just then Julie walked into the room. Angie blinked her eyes. Had Kenny really had the nerve to show up at the hospital with Julie? Angie had already thought that this was all a cruel trick that was being played on her. Now she found herself thinking that it was a cruel trick *with bonuses*. Was that possible? Memories came flooding back. She remembered all the times that she sensed that something was going on between Kenny and Julie, but she didn't want to accept it. She knew that her and Kenny's relationship was waning, but she secretly hoped that it could be mended. She kept telling herself that it would get better. She had even envisioned their life together years down the road. They would both attend college, graduate together, get married, find great jobs, buy a home and start a family. It would be a *once upon a time/happily ever after* life. They once were like a hand in a glove, but now the glove no longer fit the hand. At some point, and she wasn't quite sure when, the glove fell off and she was left cold, a hand with no covering, wishing for that glove. Now here she was, on the absolute worst day of her life, her mother clinging on by a wing and a prayer, asking herself what she had done to deserve this. Had she wronged someone in a previous life? Had she run over an animal in the street and not turned back to see if it was okay? Surely that had to be it. She couldn't recall, but whatever the reason, she felt that she was being punished in the worst kind of way. What rotten timing this was, on this day of all days, when Kenny should have been her rock, when she needed him the most. She thought of a million things that she could say to Julie, but none of those statements would make matters better. None of them would bring back what she and Kenny once had. So instead, she managed to say, "Hello Julie, thanks for coming." She knew that the best thing to do at this point was just to be cordial.

Aaron greeted Kenny with a handshake. "Thanks for coming man." Aaron did not address Julie directly, but only gave her a half smile. Angie had previously confided in Aaron that things were shaky between her and Kenny and had told him about Julie. Aaron had not cared much for Julie since she came to San Antonio South. Something about her rubbed him the wrong way. He never understood how Kenny fell head over heels for her immediately.

But that was all water under the bridge at this point and was certainly nothing to think about right now.

"Family of Pamela Burke?" the Amazon lady at the desk called out. "Right here," they all answered in unison. "The doctor will speak with you now. Please meet him in the conference room across the hall." Kenny and Julie remained in the family waiting room, while James and the twins went in to meet the doctor across the hall.

Angie and Aaron sat next to each other on one side of the table, both lost in their own thoughts. James sat across the table from them. After several long minutes, the doctor joined them. He was tall and lanky and despite the circumstances, Angie almost burst into laughter when she saw him. He looked exactly like Shaggy from Scooby Doo, one of her and Aaron's favorite cartoons. He wore a gray jacket that appeared to be one size too small, and his legs seemed to go on forever.

"I'm Dr. Milton." He extended his hand.

"Hello," Angie and Aaron said perfectly in sync. It happened all the time: another twin phenomenon. Their father managed a half nod. "Well, the good news is that Mrs. Burke is out of surgery. She had several broken bones and fractures, the worst injury being to her back. I'm going to be straightforward with you and tell you that there is a real possibility that she could be paralyzed from the waist down. Some of the vertebrae in her lower back were broken, which resulted in a spinal cord injury."

"She will need a lot of emotional support," Shaggy went on to say.

Angie thought, "Why not just provide me with a huge rock to crawl under and spend the rest of my life there? That will do just fine." But out loud she spoke for herself and Aaron and her father, "Yes, she will certainly have plenty of support." She seemed to have been appointed the spokesperson for the day. James Burke was still in somewhat of a state of shock. "We will just take it one day at a time," Angie continued. "We'll get through it." Angie looked over at Aaron and thought that he seemed to have grown much older in just the last several hours. She looked at her father and thought he will need just as much emotional support. Although she felt very small and afraid and vulnerable, she knew she had to summon some strength from somewhere. It was going to be a very long road ahead. Pamela Burke was not only her mom, but her best friend and her biggest cheerleader. She knew she now had to step up to the plate.

"Okay, then." Dr. Milton interrupted Angie's thoughts. "She will be in recovery for some time, and then transferred to intensive care. You can go in and see her if you like, but only one person at a time." They thanked the doctor as he left the room. Angie laughed to herself again as the doctor walked out. "Scooby Doobie Doo, Where Are You?" Even in the worst of situations, sometimes humor can surface.

"Are you hungry?" Aaron asked Angie and their father.

"I could use a bite," Angie answered.

Their father turned robotically and looked at both of

them. "No, I'm good." Aaron walked over and patted his father on the shoulder. "We'll grab you something, Dad. You need to eat."

The cafeteria was two floors down. As they got on the elevator, a nurse who was already on greeted them both. "How are you tonight?" she asked with a smile.

"We've been better," Angie answered.

"I understand," the nurse replied. "Just know that whatever the situation is with your loved one right now, God is a healer and a comforter."

"Thank you so much," Angie's voice caught in her throat. The elevator doors opened, and the nurse gave them a warm smile and walked quietly down the hall in the opposite direction. Angie and Aaron looked at each other. Without saying a word, they knew what each was thinking. That was just what they both needed to hear. Just a few words from a kind stranger. They both instantly felt just a little bit stronger.

The cafeteria food was surprisingly tasty. Angie didn't realize that she was as hungry as she was. However, Aaron just picked at his food. Angie's heart ached for her twin. She always teased him about eating everything in sight. His stomach was like a bottomless pit. But today he could hardly get through more than a few bites.

Angie spoke softly, "Why don't we stop by the chapel before we go back upstairs?" The next words Aaron spoke sent chills through Angie's body. "Chapel? For what? To pray to a God who did this? To say thanks a bunch for letting my mom go down in a plane?" His voice sounded oddly strange and Angie knew that he was reacting out of fear and anger. She had never seen her brother like this, but then again, it was not every day that your mom was in a plane crash. "Aaron, you can't talk like that. Yes, it's unbelievable and I wish more than anything that it was all a horrible dream, but we can't change it. I'm angry too, but Dad needs us to be strong right now. We have to do that for him." Aaron's anger seemed to subside a little bit as they walked toward the chapel.

The chapel was small and quiet with comfortable pews. There were five rows on each side and it reminded Angie of a movie she had seen years ago about some bank robbers who hid out in a hospital chapel, thinking that was the last place the police would look for them. Again, she had to chuckle to herself. That was happening a lot today. Perhaps it was just a coping mechanism. They both knelt on the stoop in front of the statue of Jesus. They held hands and closed their eyes, not knowing what to say. They prayed for strength and they prayed for their mother. When they finished their prayers, they turned to see Kenny and Julie standing in the doorway. At this point, Angie had no more fight in her. It didn't matter either way. She got up and walked past Kenny and Julie without a glance. Aaron approached them and said "I think it might be best if the two of you left. We appreciate you coming, but we're good." Kenny stared at the floor for a moment, then said, "No problem. Talk to you later."

Down the hallway, James Burke sat and waited for Angela and Aaron to return from the cafeteria. He leaned back in his seat and let his mind go back to when he and Pamela had graduated law school and started their lives together.

## CHAPTER THREE

### *(Twenty Years Earlier)*

St. Mary's University in San Antonio, Texas is one of the most prestigious law schools in the state, and anyone who received his or her Juris Doctor (law degree) from there already had a leg up when it came to being offered a job at one of the top law firms in the city — not only in San Antonio for that matter, but in the state of Texas. To even be accepted at St. Mary's you had to have ranked in the top 10 percentile of your graduating college class. James was nervously preparing for the most exciting day of his life. Today was the commencement exercise at St.

Mary's, where he would be receiving his law degree. He only wished that his parents were here to witness it. James was an only child. His mother and father had divorced when he was three years old, and he could remember growing up and only seeing his father a few times a year. When he became old enough to understand, he found out that his mother had sole custody and his father was back and forth with the court system trying to obtain the right to have shared custody of his son. As he later came to find out, his father had a substance abuse problem and therefore the court granted sole custody of James to his mother. He always enjoyed the time that he was able to spend with his father. In the eyes of a child, his father could do no wrong. They both loved sports, old cars, going camping, and hiking. He always looked forward to his father coming to visit, but ultimately it would always end up with his parents having an argument. That was the downside. He wondered why it was so hard for two people that shared a child to get along. He promised himself that if he ever got married and had children, he would do everything in his power to make sure that the marriage did not end in divorce. He thought it was very selfish of a mother and father to divorce. He thought they should consider the effect it would have on a child and do all they could to make the marriage work. But now of course as an adult, he realized that was not the way it worked. In the end, his father had remarried a Nigerian woman and moved halfway around the world. James and his father had eventually grown apart and he only heard from his father periodically. He had contacted him to tell him that he was graduating law school and his father only sent a note saying, "Congratulations." So that was the end of that. James decided he would not reach out to him anymore. Funny how life worked sometimes.

His mother had developed Alzheimer's and was now living in a long-term care facility. James knew it would be pointless to even attempt to let her know what was going on. The events of his childhood had been his motivation for wanting to become an attorney and advocate for fathers' rights. Even though he and his father were now estranged, he still remembered how wonderful it felt when they had their visits, and he wished that his father could have had shared custody. He was not sure at this point if that would have made a difference in the outcome of things, but sometimes the slightest detour can determine where you ultimately end up in life.

"James Burke, Esquire. Sounds good to me." James turned

to see Pamela standing in the doorway. "I didn't hear you come in," he said and smiled as he kissed her lightly on the cheek.

"You were in very deep thought." Pamela seemed concerned. "Is something wrong? I can't imagine you could be anything but smiles today. After all, it is *OUR* big day," she said and smiled brightly. James looked at Pamela and his heart melted. It happened every time she flashed that huge smile. He could be having the worst day ever, but she was always a ray of sunshine. He was so thankful for her. She always knew just the right words to say in any situation. She was his best friend, his rock, his voice of reason. And she was soon to be his wife. That was the icing on the cake.

"I'm fine," he smiled back at her. "I was just thinking about my mom and dad. But you're right, this is *OUR* big day and only smiles are in order."

Pamela was also graduating from St. Mary's School of Law. She and James had been high school sweethearts, had attended the same college, and had both decided to pursue a degree in law. While James concentrated in the area of Family Law, Pamela went in a totally different direction and made Real Estate her specialty. She had always been fascinated with building and zoning laws and regulations.

She had grown up in a small town in Iowa, and her father had owned a general store as well as the lot adjacent to it. She and her older sister, Regina, loved to help out at the store. When they were old enough, their father would let them work the cash register and paid them a small salary. When her father's health started to decline and he was no longer able to run the store, Pamela wished she would have been old enough to take over the business. She was fascinated with the idea of someday owning commercial real estate or at least working in that field. Regina, on the other hand, vowed that she would never settle down anywhere. They were polar opposites.

Regina aspired to become a runway model. She totally had the looks for it; she was tall and slender with long legs and flawless skin. She was a free spirit. After their father's decision to close the store, their mother had no interest in continuing to run the store, and so they decided to sell the property and move to San Antonio. At first Pamela was horrified at the idea of living anywhere else other than the familiar surroundings where she had lived most of her life. But she quickly adapted to San Antonio, especially after meeting James on the first day at her new high school. They had become fast friends, and soon were inseparable. There was a definite attraction, and slowly the friendship turned into a monogamous relationship. They spent as many waking hours together as possible. They found that they had a lot in common. They both enjoyed the same kind of music; they both liked sports, especially football; and they both could eat ice cream for breakfast, lunch and dinner. James once joked that the ice cream fetish was enough reason for them to get married and grow old together. They complemented each other perfectly to a tee, and even finished each other's sentences. It was a match made in heaven.

The commencement ceremony was less than an hour away, and both James and Pamela were eager to finally come to the end of a long road that had started so many years ago. They walked the short distance across the campus to the arena where the graduation was being held. Hundreds of students and their friends and families were gathering outside the building. There was such a feeling of jubilation and celebration. The graduates were being directed to enter through the auditorium door to prepare for the start of the ceremony.

"We did it," James said, smiling at Pamela.

"Yes, we did," Pamela said and  smiled back. "It's so surreal, but here we are. Let's get this done."

Pamela's mother and her sister Regina gave her one last hug before she joined the other graduates. "I'm so proud of you," her mom said as her eyes brimmed with tears.

"Mom, please save the tears for later," Regina laughed. They all laughed at her remark. That was typical of Regina.

"I only wish your father could be here," her mother said as a somber look passed over her face. Her father's health had deteriorated rapidly after they left Iowa, and he had passed away from a brain aneurysm within one year after moving to San Antonio.

"Well he is here in spirit, and we all know how proud he would be," James quickly reminded them as he squeezed Pamela's hand. James was always so reassuring, always the one to diffuse any awkward situation. Pamela loved him for that.

"All right, you two, hurry in before they close the doors and there will be no graduation for you." Regina laughed. They all exchanged one last hug before James and Pamela disappeared into the auditorium.

The celebration following the graduation was massive. There were tables lining the walls filled with food and drinks. Everyone stayed and enjoyed the festivities late into the afternoon. James was one of the most popular law students at St. Mary's. Pamela thought he looked like a candidate campaigning for office as he went through the room talking to all of his fellow graduates. She smiled just watching him. He always had that effect on her.

"We will be the last ones to leave for sure," Regina quipped, "Mr. President has to make his rounds." Again, typical Regina, and again Pamela and her mother burst into laughter.

Finally, the afternoon came to an end. James and Pamela were now "official" and it was the best feeling in the world. Life was grand, despite some losses, but their best days were ahead of them. As they all walked toward the car, Regina announced "Well I hate to break up this grand celebration, but my private jet awaits."

"In your dreams," Pamela laughed.

"Okay, well I'm speaking it into existence." Regina tried to look serious. "For now, I will have to settle for coach, but you'll see." She was leaving for a week-long trip to Atlanta where she would be meeting with a top modeling agency. She had graduated college two years earlier, receiving a degree in Business Management. She planned to open her own modeling school, and so far, she was on track to doing so. Her feet had barely touched ground since she finished college. She was a true jetsetter already. She was smart and sassy and had a good head on her shoulders.

"Have a safe flight and be careful," her mom said, smiling. Regina's color would be Red. It was true that no matter how many children you have, they all can be so different. She only had two girls, but they were as different as night and day, oil and water, black and white. The year after she graduated college, Regina had spontaneously had her hair dyed fire engine red, and after that, her family nicknamed her "Red." While Pamela was blue — quiet, structured, and serious, Regina was red — very vocal, spontaneous, and quite the prankster.

The summer seemed to come and go in a flash. Both James and Pamela passed the bar exam with flying colors. It was September, and the weather was starting to change. The leaves were falling, and the colors were vibrant and bright. Even though the leaves were dying as they changed colors, it was still a beautiful sight. God's masterpiece. Amazing how He can brighten up even a dead situation. James and Pamela were both extremely busy beginning their careers, but still found time to plan for a December wedding. It would be a small ceremony, with only family and a few close friends. Both their families were small, so it would be an easy undertaking. They planned to rent a small venue and have the ceremony and reception at the same place.

They were married on Christmas Eve. The wedding went off without a hitch. There was one bridesmaid and one groomsman, and a maid of honor and a best man. Even though the weather was not cold, the bridesmaids wore hand muffs instead of carrying flowers, since it was a December wedding. The flower girl dropped tiny flowers in the shape of snowflakes. The hand muffs and snowflake flowers were Pamela's mother's idea, and all the guests thought it was quite ingenious. Tiny ceramic Christmas trees served as centerpieces on each table. The room was decorated ever so delicately with mistletoe and garland. Pamela wore a winter white gown with hints of glitter. It was a simple A-line dress with a modest train. In her hand she carried a red, green, and silver bouquet comprised of tiny Christmas ornaments. A medley of holiday music played softly during the processional and throughout the reception. James was as handsome as ever in a black tuxedo with a cream cummerbund, vest, and bow tie. It was a picture-perfect ceremony.

They honeymooned in Hawaii during the week between Christmas and New Year's. Then it was back to the grind in January. By now, James had a solid client base. He enjoyed his work helping fathers gain the right to equal time with their children. It was not glamorous work, but very satisfying. There was such a sense of accomplishment and gratification each time the judge granted shared or equal custody. He still remembered how he felt when he could not spend time with his father. So many lost opportunities that could never be recovered. But at least this was his way of giving back and sparing children the hurt he had endured.

Meanwhile, Pamela was becoming quite the superstar at

her firm. She had hit the ground running. She loved everything about her job. She could never get enough of building and zoning, land use, and property law. The more complicated the deal, the more she thrived. Within two years because of her track record, she was promoted to junior partner and then after just five years, she was named senior partner.

Pamela Burke couldn't ask for a better life.

# CHAPTER FOUR

"Mr. Burke." The doctor interrupted James' thoughts. "Your wife is out of recovery and in ICU now if you would like to see her. But please, only one person at a time for ten minutes each." Angie and Aaron both looked at their father. He had been lost in his thoughts, and now he looked at the doctor as if his words were taking a minute to register.

"Sure, yes, I'll go in now."

"Okay, fine," the doctor replied. "Just beyond the nurse's station, they will direct you."

As James entered the room, he was not prepared for what he saw. Pamela lay motionless with tubes attached to her face and arms. A monitor was beeping softly as it measured her vital signs. She had several bruises on her face and neck and her eyes appeared swollen. He softly stroked her hand and began to cry. He wished that he could take her place. He would have given anything to not have her lying there. Although he was not sure if she could hear him, he leaned over and whispered in her ear. "Remember our wedding vows, for better or worse. I'm here and I'm not going home without you."

It might have been his imagination, but he could have sworn that Pamela moved her hand. At least that's what he chose to believe. He sat on the side of the bed looking closely at her face for any signs of movement. He watched her sleeping and thought that even after surviving a plane crash and undergoing hours of surgery, she still looked beautiful. "For better or worse, in sickness and health, for richer or poorer, forsaking all others, 'til death do us part." It seemed only yesterday that he had spoken those words. Rest assured, at some point every last word of those wedding vows will come into play. Now "in sickness and in health" was here. It had arrived with a vengeance and without warning. It had come hard and fast like a sudden rainstorm, unmistakable and undeniable. Just then, a nurse quietly entered the room and told James that he would have to leave. He kissed his wife on the forehead and went back to where Angie and Aaron were waiting.

"How is she?" they asked at once.

"She's coming along. But why don't you all wait a little while and then take your turn to go in?"

"No problem," came the one voice.

Angie absolutely detested hospitals. Just the sight and smell depressed her. Now she had to walk not only into a hospital room, but one where her mother was lying. She stood close to her mother's bedside and again couldn't control the tears. If she had a dollar for each tear she had cried today, she would be a millionaire ten times over. She leaned over and gently kissed her mother on the head.

"I love you, mom," she said softly. There were few, if any, words that could be said right now. She sat in the chair next to the bed and leaned back. She had never felt so tired. She decided to close her eyes for the ten minutes that she would spend in the room. As often is the case when a loved one is extremely ill, memories started to fill Angie's head. She could never recall her mother even having so much as a head cold. She was always vibrant and healthy. Pamela was the glue that held the Burke family together, and she did it seemingly with ease. Angie always admired her mother for her strength. She often mused to Aaron that she didn't know how their mom kept up with work and home, especially with raising twins.

She remembered how mischievous they had been while growing up. When they were about two years old, they realized that there were two of them and that if they ran in two different directions, their mother could only chase one of them. She wasn't sure how, but she even remembered being in a playpen with her brother. She would stand and bang against the sides to try to make their mother pick her up. Aaron, on the other hand, seemed quite content to be jailed. She once joked that he had criminal instincts even as a toddler.

Angie and Aaron had always been on the A/B Honor Roll throughout grade school and high school. They both had a love for reading, perhaps because their mom or dad read to them every night before they even learned to read, and when they were old enough, took them to the library every Saturday. It was a requirement that they each read two books every week, from cover to cover, in addition to their homework and household chores. But since the twins had such a love for learning, it came easy for them.

The doctor had informed them that Pamela could possibly be paralyzed from the accident. Angie thought back to when they were young children, and their mother would play in the backyard with them. They had a swing set and a pool in the backyard. Angie and Aaron never got enough of playing on the swings and sliding board. They played volleyball in the pool, and of course, living in Texas, it was pretty much warm all year round so the entire family enjoyed the pool. They would grill in the backyard on weekends and sometimes invite neighbors over for a late lunch. It was an idyllic life indeed. Even when they became teenagers, their parents would still join them in a game of volleyball. Now there would be no more volleyball for her mother. Angie didn't miss not having a sister. Her mother was her big sister, as well as her best friend. They would have mother-daughter talks and Angie knew she could tell her anything without being judged. She might not have always gotten the answer she wanted, but she knew her mother would never steer her wrong.

Angie heard footsteps and then felt a hand tap lightly on her shoulder. "I'm sorry, dear," the nurse spoke in a whisper. "You will have to leave now."

As she opened her eyes and looked around, Angie realized that she had dozed off more deeply than she knew. She looked over at the bed where her mother was still lying hooked up to tubes and monitors. Again came the tears, and again in spite of the horrific circumstances, a hint of humor. Angie half smiled through the tears as she thought to herself, "Someone must have a remote control that keeps turning on the tears every hour on the hour. Yes, that has to be it."

She stood up to leave and touched her mother's hand again. Pamela Burke was not the strong one at this moment. Pamela Burke could not move her arms or legs. If only she could just open her eyes and flash that beautiful smile and wink at Angie as she often did when they shared a secret only between the two of them.

James would sometimes see them exchange a look and say, "Uh oh...I don't know what you two are cooking up, but it can't be good."

Aaron would say in his usual joking manner, "Dad, I would sleep with one eye open if I were you. You gotta watch the quiet ones." They would all burst into laughter.

"You'll have to go now, sweetie, I'm sorry," the nurse gently prompted Angie again. She took one last look at her mother and left the room.

As she walked back down the hall to where Aaron and her father had been sitting, she saw that Aaron had his eyes closed. He had dozed off in the comfortable chair.

"Well, I guess we all need that," she said to her father as she looked over at Aaron. She sat down in the chair on the other side of her father. "Dad," she touched his arm, "I still can't believe this is happening. But we will get through this. We have to."

James looked at his daughter. Even though she was only 17 years old, she seemed so adult and so mature right now. All parents try to raise their children to become responsible adults. It wasn't always easy, but as he looked at Angie, he was proud of the woman she was becoming. "I know we will, sweetie, I know," he answered. He glanced over at Aaron who was now snoring softly. "Maybe I can join him in that dream."

Angie laughed at her father's remark. She was grateful that for the first time in the last several hours he had managed a full smile and now even a laugh. Angie could only imagine how difficult this was for her dad: to have things going along smoothly one minute and then tragedy strike the next minute. Now the long days and nights that were ahead loomed large in Angie's mind. They all had their own unique relationship with her mom. To James she was his childhood sweetheart, his wife, his closest ally, his confidante and always the voice of reason.

She wondered what was going through her dad's mind. She wondered what was happening in Aaron's dream. She thought about the other people who were involved in the crash and their loved ones, and said a silent prayer for them. Some of the family members had been in the cafeteria when she and Aaron were there. It was so surreal; they were all suddenly members of a club that no one wanted to join, initiated in against their will, unable to opt out.

Aaron involuntarily jerked and sat up quickly. He had just had one of those dreams that everyone has at some point where someone is chasing you and is closing in on you. But just before they catch up with you, you wake up. Aaron enjoyed the study of psychology and psychoanalysis. He now remembered reading in a *Huffington Post* series on dreams and their meanings, that Dr. Richard Nicolette, J.D., a psychotherapist trained at the Jung Institute in Boston, explained that dreaming that you are being chased generally means that you are being told by your subconscious that you are avoiding an issue or a person. You are avoiding something painful, annoying, or fearful.

"Well, the good doctor was certainly on point," Aaron thought to himself as he straightened up in the chair. All of those adjectives applied to what he was feeling at this moment. But now he had to face the music. He had to face the fact that this was not a dream with a subliminal meaning or explanation. This was him sitting next to his twin sister Angie and his father in a family waiting room at Bayside Medical with his mother in ICU just down the hall. This was by far the worst day of his life. What had started as a normal day at school had ended being an episode of "Grey's Anatomy," only the doctors were not actors. It was not Dr. Grey and Dr. Bailey, although Shaggy had made a cameo appearance in this episode. No, this was real life. No matter how badly he wanted someone to jump out and say "you've been punked," that was not happening. He would even have gladly accepted that it was a sick joke and would have forgiven the person who played it on him. He closed his eyes for a few more seconds before standing up to walk down the hall to the room where his mother was.

# CHAPTER FIVE

Pamela Burke lay in the hospital bed, surrounded by tubes and beeping monitors and sterile instruments. She was starting to come out from under the anesthesia, but not yet fully awake. It would be several hours before she would be coherent enough to speak, but she could faintly hear voices. Although drifting in and out of consciousness, she heard James when he came in and spoke to her. She could feel the love in his voice and the touch of his hand. She heard Angela and felt her presence as she sat near her bedside.

Anesthetic dreaming occurs during recovery when patients are sedated or in a physiologic sleep state. Such was the case with Pamela Burke. In her dreams, Pamela saw Aaron and Angela when they were five years old, heading out for their first day of school. Angie looked timid and afraid, while Aaron was ready to take on the world. He promised to take care of his little sister. Pamela drove them to school for the very first day, and as they walked through the doors, she couldn't hold back the tears. Her babies were leaving her for the first time, and it was overwhelming. She wondered if every parent felt this way on the very first day of school. In conversations with some of her friends, she had heard them talk about how anxious they felt on their child's first day of kindergarten. There was no feeling that compared to that very first day.

The next day they were picked up by the school bus. She walked them all the way out to the bus so that she could meet the driver. He was an elderly gentleman, perhaps in his early sixties. Pamela guessed he was most likely retired. That gave her some comfort because she thought he would be a very careful driver and good with the children.

"Good Morning," she greeted the driver.

"Good Morning, Ma'am," he smiled. As if reading her mind, he said "Don't worry, they will be fine. We're all family on here." He motioned toward the middle of the bus where a woman was ushering the twins to their seat. "Mary, come up here for a quick second, honey."

The woman got the twins seated and put their seat belts on and then made her way to the front.

"Good Morning," she said, smiling. Just as with the driver, Pamela felt immediately comforted by her greeting. "This is my wife, Mary," the driver went on to say. "My name is Frank, and we've been driving this bus route for about three years."

"Twins?" Mary asked Pamela.

"Yes they are," Pamela answered and smiled back.

"Well, trust me, they will be fine. We watch out for all our children on this bus. We never drive off until we see them go inside the house. We've never experienced any problems."

"Thank you so much." Pamela breathed a sigh of relief. She was grateful that she had decided to take off work the first week of school. She knew she would have been far too anxious to have been at the office. Besides, she had just closed on a huge property and so her workload would be lighter now for another week or so.

Pamela's mind drifted in and out of sleep. Now she saw Red at the twins' 10th birthday party.

"I really wish you would not spend money so lavishly on them," she scolded Red. "They have way too many things already."

"Oh Pam, lighten up," Red retorted. "I think I should be able to spend as much money on them as I like." James was standing in earshot and Red shot him a glance. He was not about to get in the middle of an argument between two sisters. It was a recurring disagreement that went on every time Red paraded in with a cart full of outlandish gifts for the children.

"It's not that you can't buy them whatever you like," Pam would say. "It's just that James and I feel that it is just too much."

"Well, I don't hear him complaining," Red snapped. Pamela finally realized she was fighting a losing battle.

James once told her, "You know there's not a lot we can do

or say about Red's behavior," and Pam had to agree. Even though they knew it was done out of love, they still felt it could have been toned down a bit. On the twins' 16th birthday, Red arrived with a diamond tennis bracelet for Angie and a belt with a diamond buckle for Aaron. Later that night, Pamela and Red had a very heated argument about the gifts. Again, Pamela thought it was just way overboard. They were talking very loudly in the kitchen when Angie walked in.

"Is something wrong?" Angie looked confused.

"No, everything's fine sweetheart," Pam assured her. Red shot a knowing look at Pam before leaving the room.

"Happy Birthday Princess," she said and kissed Angie on the cheek.

Aaron noticed his mother slightly stirring when he entered her room. Perhaps she had been dreaming. He wanted so badly for her to be able to see him. He wished that he didn't have to see her like this. It all seemed so unfair, so unbalanced. Why did bad things happen to good people? He already knew the answer to that question. He knew that no one was exempt from trouble and it did not matter whether he or she was a "good" person or a "bad" person. That was life and God is in control of all life. He also knew that it could have been so much worse. So he sat next to the bed and he closed his eyes. He was thankful that his mother was still alive and that he could spend just a few minutes with her. Aaron thought about all the times when he was growing up and his parents would take them on outings, mostly to local attractions. It didn't have to be big and fancy: just trips out for ice cream, to the zoo, the aquarium and planetarium. His mother always seemed to enjoy the attractions as much as Aaron and Angela did. On one of their trips to the zoo, Aaron became so enthralled with the giraffes that he did not realize that his parents and Angie were walking away. He stood there continuing to communicate with the giraffes. A moment later, James noticed that Aaron was not by his side. He started to panic when Pam said calmly, "Hold on, I know just where he is."

She walked back to where they had just left the giraffe exhibit and there was Aaron, still standing there with his face pressed against the bars totally fascinated by the giraffes. Aaron was torn between whether he wanted to study medicine or veterinary science in college. Angie often teased him "Well, either you work with two-legged animals or four-legged animals. Your choice."

The family often went on picnics, which was Aaron's favorite thing to do because he could eat non-stop. He didn't know how she did it, but his mother always packed a picnic basket that seemed to never be empty. He didn't know how she did a lot of things, but her family was always taken care of. They never missed a meal and never wanted for anything. And then there was Aunt Red. Always there for birthdays and Christmas, bearing gifts. He once said that he and Angie were lucky to have two moms. He looked again at his mother and thanked God that she had survived. He had been angry at first, but now he knew that he had so much to be thankful for.

"I'm so sorry, I didn't mean to startle you," the nurse apologized as she walked in. Aaron didn't realize he had been so deeply lost in his thoughts. His time was up with his mother, but he didn't want to leave. He would have stayed longer or even overnight if he could, but he knew that would not be allowed. So he slowly stood and reluctantly left the room.

# CHAPTER SIX

Pamela was released from the hospital after six days. It had been confirmed that she was paralyzed from the waist down and would need a wheelchair. She was equipped with a top of the line motorized chair. She was on a couple of medications to manage the pain, but that was the easy part compared to what lay ahead. James put plans in motion immediately to bring in contractors to remodel the kitchen and bathroom so that they would be wheelchair accessible. Luckily, they lived in a one-story home so there were no stairs to worry about.

James also hired caretakers to assist Pamela for the first few months. It was a huge undertaking and the whole family had to get used to the new way of living. Going from living normally one day to being paralyzed the next was unthinkable. When the doctor first gave her the diagnosis, Pamela was in shock and disbelief. She stared at him blankly, trying to digest what he had told her.

James was there holding her hand, but all she heard was the word "paralyzed" and her mind couldn't accept it. She looked at James as if he were a complete stranger. She didn't remember hearing anything else that was said after that. On her first day home, she just lay in bed and cried as reality started to set in. She had no appetite for a few days, and she found herself wishing that she would not have even survived. It was a horrible thought, but it crossed her mind more than once. The doctor had actually cautioned James to keep her medications out of her reach, because it was not uncommon for patients with paralysis to contemplate suicide, and an overdose would be the easiest way out. She started snapping at the caretakers when they tried to help her with bathing and dressing. She knew she could not do it alone yet — not until after much therapy, which was months down the road — but she still took out her anger and frustration on them. She started to become cold and distant with James. He had the patience of Job and he loved his wife to no end, but some days it even started to get next to him.

James had contacted Red when the accident first occurred. She was in Milan but said that she would get there as soon as possible. On the second day after Pamela came home, Red arrived. This time of course there were no gifts, but still in typical Red fashion, there was pomp and circumstance from the minute she stepped out of the limousine. She rushed in like a whirlwind and ran straight in the direction of Pamela's bedroom.

"Oh my God, Pam! I couldn't believe it when I heard the news. I got here as soon as I could. Thank goodness you are all right."

Pam was glad see her sister, but she didn't want her to make a fuss. She was still trying to adjust mentally and physically. Red stayed for a week, and James was thankful for the distraction. The whole situation had taken quite a toll on him.

A couple of times he had gone out for dinner after work with some of his colleagues. When he got home, Pam was furious and complained that he had left her alone. James couldn't believe what he heard. "Alone? What do you mean alone? The caretakers are here, the kids are here."

"But you're my husband," Pamela sounded like a very insecure woman, something that was totally out of her character. "You should be here with me."

James walked over to where she was sitting. "Pam, you know how much I love you. This is not easy for me either, but —"

Before he could finish his sentence, Pam practically screamed, "No James! You have no idea how it feels not to be able to move, to be totally helpless and have to wait for someone to do everything for you. My days feel like an eternity. I don't even know one day from the next."

James kept his voice steady and said, "Sweetheart, I've done all I can to make the house comfortable for you. I've made sure you are well cared for. I haven't taken on any extra cases at work so that I can have more time at home. What else do you want me to do?"

"I want you to come home!" Pam shrieked. "I want you to come home and not go out with whoever you have been leaving work with!" James looked at his wife in disbelief. Whoever he had been leaving work with? Did she really just say that? Exactly what was she insinuating? James decided the best thing to do at this point was just walk away and let Pam calm down and gather her thoughts. He didn't want to fight fire with fire and his nerves were still on edge as well. Caring for some who is incapacitated was more than a notion. He walked down the hall to the kitchen.

Angie and Aaron were there and when they saw him, they immediately knew something was wrong. The bedroom door had been closed, but they could hear their mother raising her voice. It wasn't the first time. She had scolded the caretakers loudly for the slightest misstep. She had been very vocal on phone calls with her co-workers who had to call with questions about some of her cases. Of course they knew and understood the cause, but instead of getting better, she seemed to be getting worse. Angie wondered if she would ever have her mother back. Once when she tried to have a conversation with her, Pamela had said "I'm sorry Angie, but I'm just not up to talking about anything." She was cutting off her family without realizing it.

Aaron was having a really tough time with the whole situation. He confided in his father that he felt he was losing communication with his mother. He was a momma's boy, but now he couldn't even get close to her.

James had told him to just give it more time, that she would get better.

As the weeks progressed, Pamela went through several different stages. She became generally mad at the world. She got stronger physically and was able to navigate her way through the house. She was able to use the special bath seat and take her own shower, but she still needed help getting dressed. A physical therapist came to the home three days a week to do lower body exercises with her. She barked at him the whole time he was there and some days refused to cooperate.

One week, a different therapist showed up. He said that the other one had asked to be unassigned from Pamela. The second therapist lasted about a month, and then he was gone as well. After that, a middle-aged woman was sent to work with Pamela. She was very mild-mannered. When Pamela raised her voice at her, she only smiled and said "It's okay, Mrs. Burke. I understand." Nothing seemed to phase her. Eventually Pamela started to look forward to the therapist's visits. James thought she was an angel and told her as much one day.

"Mr. Burke," she said and smiled. "I've done this for many years and I've never had a patient that I couldn't handle. I realize how tough it is. I pray during my therapy sessions. I ask God to let me be a comfort to the person I am working with. You see, Mr. Burke, God doesn't make mistakes. While it's tragic what happened to your wife, it was still in divine order. We can't see it. Your wife certainly can't see it. She is hurt and angry. But there is a blessing in everything that we go through."

"Thank you," James' voice was shaky. "We are all learning and adjusting through this whole thing. I'm so glad you're here."

## CHAPTER SEVEN

Regina Taylor had always been a free spirit. She was a rambunctious child, but yet well behaved. Growing up in a small town in Iowa, she always dreamed of one day becoming a professional model and traveling the world. When the family moved to San Antonio, Texas, in her junior year in high school, she got her first taste of modeling. She entered a local beauty contest and won first place.

She was a naturally beautiful girl. Not only that, but she was a straight A student. Her sister, Pamela, was just the opposite. Quiet and reserved, Pamela preferred staying far away from the limelight. After graduating high school, Regina earned her B.A. in Business Management. She was wise enough to know that she could not retire off of good looks and long legs. Her long-range goal was to open a professional modeling school.

After college, Regina's career took off. She started to make the right connections. She was approached by a well-known modeling agency located in Atlanta. They asked her to come out for an interview. When she arrived, she was awestruck with the agency. It was on the top floor of a building in downtown Atlanta in the business district on Peachtree Street. The furnishings were immaculate. Even the front desk receptionist looked as if she had just stepped off the cover of Vogue Magazine. All of the employees, both men and women, looked picture perfect: not a hair out of place. She sat in the waiting area along with four other young women, all hoping to be hired on at the agency. They all looked flawless from head to toe with perfectly done manicures and make up. For the first time in her life, Regina felt just a bit insecure. But this was the real world, far away from the little town in Iowa or San Antonio. This was it. Sink or swim. And she totally intended to swim — butterfly, backstroke, and freestyle.

"Regina Taylor?" the receptionist called out. "Mrs. Mason will see you now." She was ushered into an office just beyond the reception desk.

"Hello, Regina, I'm Kelly Mason." Regina extended her hand.

"Nice to meet you Mrs. Mason," Regina replied nervously.

"Please, have a seat." She motioned toward a plush chair in front of her desk. Kelly Mason was unbelievably beautiful. Regina thought to herself, this will be me one day, sitting on the other side of this desk, still beautiful after a successful modeling career and ready to help other women who are just starting out.

Kelly Mason began, "I've looked at your portfolio and let me say that I'm very impressed. You're extremely photogenic and I see you've had some exposure already."

"Thank you," Regina replied. "I'm proud of my accomplishments."

Mrs. Mason continued, "I see in some of your photos that your hair was a beautiful shade of red. I think that color looks absolutely gorgeous with your skin. Would you be opposed to wearing your hair that color again? We do use wigs and hair pieces in some of our photo shoots, but in others we want the models to wear their own hair."

Regina laughed out loud, "I would have no problem with the red hair, not at all. I'm laughing because when I dyed my hair that color a couple of years ago, I acquired the nickname "Red" from my family."

Mrs. Mason smiled brightly, "I like you already, Regina. I think we have our newest model. You certainly have the look and the credentials. And we will call you 'Red.'"

*Sunrise, sunset. Sunrise, sunset. Swiftly fly the years.* Red quickly became known as one of the hottest models in the business. She worked with such names as Gigi Hadid, Tyra Banks, Gisele Bundchen, Naomi Campbell, and seasoned professional, Cindy Crawford. She was one of the most sought-after models in the U.S. and Europe. If Red was seen wearing a certain style, that designer's sales skyrocketed. Fashion houses competed for her. She appeared on the cover of dozens of magazines and was named Model of the Year for three consecutive years.

On a week-long photo shoot in Paris, Red managed to carve out some alone time on the last night there. Paris was such a beautiful city. This was her third trip there, and she never grew tired of it. She loved the sights and sounds, the beautiful architecture and, of course, the Eiffel Tower. As she strolled along the Champ de Mars, she decided to stop at one of the street side bistros for coffee. She ordered Un Café Crème, which is coffee blended with milk. That was her favorite. It reminded her of her childhood when her mother used to let her and her sister drink egg nog at Christmastime. No matter where in the world she traveled or how many famous people she rubbed elbows with, her heart was still at home. She loved her family, and visited whenever she got the chance.

As she sipped on her coffee, a gentleman approached her. She was fully prepared to give him her autograph. Her face was well known in Paris, and people often asked for her autograph, and she was always glad to oblige. Even with her immense fame, she remained humble. That is just who she was.

"Excusez moi, Madame," he said, his voice like butter. Red was caught off-guard. She looked up to see the most handsome man she had ever laid eyes on. "Would you mind if I joined you?"

"Of course," Red answered.

"Hello," he said and extended his hand. "I'm Alexandre Armand."

"Regina Taylor," she shook his hand. "Nice to meet you."

"Oh, you're American?" He looked surprised.

"Yes, I am," Red smiled. "That surprises you?"

"Yes." He flashed a smile. "But please don't take offense. I meant no harm. It's just that I don't see many Americans dining alone around here. They are usually in couples or groups.

"Well, I'm not exactly alone," Red continued. "I'm here working, and just decided to spend some time alone to relax." "Well, then, I didn't mean to disturb you. I'll let you get back to your thoughts," he turned to leave.

"No, it's fine. Please, join me," Red invited him to sit. He had definitely gotten her attention, and she instantly wanted to know more about him. He hadn't seemed to recognize who she was, so that in itself let her know that he was not a fan who just wanted an autograph and a photo op, even though she never minded that. But something about him intrigued her.

"Thank you." He flashed the winning smile again. The waiter approached the table and Alexandre ordered Un Café Serré, a strong, bitter blend of coffee.

"He's definitely French," Red mused. "That stuff will put hair on your chest."

"So," Alexandre continued, "What brings you to Paris, if I may ask?"

"I'm here for a photo shoot," Red replied. "Actually, this is my last evening here."

"Photo shoot? So you are with a modeling company?"

"Yes, I am." When she told him the name, Alexandre looked a little embarrassed as he replied, "I've heard of that agency, but I must confess that I did not recognize you. I'm not very familiar with the fashion industry."

"No need to apologize," Red laughed. Alexandre looked like a little mischievous boy that had gotten caught red-handed.

"I love your laugh," Alexandre smiled at Red.

"Thank you." Red blushed. Alexandre's smile faded for a quick second.

"I'm so sorry this is your last night here. I guess that's my rotten luck. Do you know if your travels will bring you back to Paris?"

"Not that I know of, but it's quite possible." Red suddenly felt sad. This total stranger that she had met only ten minutes ago now had her full attention and she knew that she wanted to see him again.

He was feeling the same thing when he said, "Would I be too forward to ask for your number? Or can I give you mine? I would love to keep in touch. Maybe we could meet here again for coffee." They both laughed at the thought of that. Somehow the way he said it just sounded funny.

"Alexandre, I would love to keep in touch," Red said. "Why don't we exchange numbers?"

"That would be wonderful," Alexandre beamed. "And by the way, please call me Alex."

"Absolutely," Red smiled. "But only if you will call me Red."

Alex called Red the very next week. When she hung up, she couldn't believe they had talked for over an hour. He told her all about his life in Paris. He was born and raised there, attended the University of Kent — School of Architecture and Planning, earning a degree in Architectural Engineering. He said that he wanted to one day move to the United States and join an engineering firm. They both laughed when Red told him that she had thought one day of moving to Paris to look into opening her own modeling agency.

There were so many parallels between them. He had one brother; Red had one sister. They were both born in the same year, within months of each other. He loved traveling, and so did Red. They both loved the opera and shopping. They talked a couple of times a week and learned more and more about each other. Finally, Alex invited Red to visit him in Paris, and she agreed to arrange to visit him in January when she would be on a furlough from the agency.

On her trip home for Christmas that year, Red told Pam all about Alex. Pam was thrilled for her sister. Red told her that she planned to visit him in January, and they would see how things went from there.

"He must be pretty special," Pam remarked. "Because Miss Globetrotter Red doesn't give anyone a second glance." It was true. Red was not the type to be tied down to one person. No grass grew under her feet. Besides, her modeling career was so demanding, she didn't have time to form any serious relationships.

When she was in James and Pamela's wedding three years ago, a good friend of James' was attracted to her. But she politely turned him down, because she knew that it would not be fair to even go out on a date with him because she traveled so many months out of the year. Settling down was not on her radar for quite some time. She admired her sister and hoped one day to have that life for herself, but right now it was not in the cards. She knew that Pamela was trying to conceive, but so far she had been unsuccessful.

"Just keep trying, sis," she had told her. "It will happen for you when you least expect it."

"I sure hope so," Pam replied. She and James had a wonderful life. The only thing missing was children, but they were still holding out hope.

Red spent the entire month of January in Paris. Alex showed her all the highlights of the city. They had coffee at the same bistro where they had first met. They talked for hours on end about things that interested them both. They took long strolls along the Seine River from the Tuileries all the way to the Bastille. They toured the quaysides, the islands, the left bank and the right bank. They stood near beautiful arched bridges and watched people fishing and mallard ducks circling in the water. They took pictures standing underneath the Eiffel Tower. They were inseparable for the entire time Red was there.

After returning home, Red was on cloud nine. She had never felt like this about anyone. Alex had shown her such a good time in Paris, and they were already planning his visit to Atlanta. Of course, it paled in comparison to Paris, but he was excited about coming to visit. Over the next few months Red and Alex still spent as much time together on the phone as they could, but her job was very demanding.

In April, Red was called on to be the lead model for an upcoming photo shoot. When she went in for wardrobe fitting, the size she normally wore was snug on her. "It must just be the designer," she told the assistant.

"Let's try the same size from another line." The wardrobe assistant brought out several size four outfits for Red to try on. They all were a tight fit. "Why don't you take five and come back in a few minutes," Red told the assistant.

Red sat down on the couch in the fitting room. She suddenly felt sick to her stomach. She closed her eyes and started to put two and two together. She had not been feeling well for a few weeks and her appetite was not the same. She had not thought anything strange because she was always irregular anyway. But this time she knew it felt different. As the gravity of situation started to set in, she felt like the room was spinning around her. She held on tight to the couch. She was still sitting in same spot when the wardrobe assistant returned. "Are you all right, Ms. Taylor?" the assistant looked concerned. "I'm fine," Red replied. "But I'm going to need to take the afternoon off."

"Well, Ms. Taylor, it looks like you're going to be a mother." The doctor smiled at Red. Red sat on the table and couldn't believe her ears.

"Are you sure?" she asked the doctor, although she already knew the answer.

"Ninety-nine percent sure, the doctor replied. "And I've been doing this for over 20 years. You don't look happy. Is everything okay?"

"It will be," Red replied dryly. "It will be."

Red called Alex that night to tell him the news. She wasn't sure how he was going to react. She only hoped that it would not destroy their relationship. They could discuss what they wanted to do going forward.

"Hey beautiful, how's it going?" Alex was his usual jovial self. "I'm good, Alex. But I have something important to talk to you about and I want to get right to the point. I saw my doctor today and found out that I'm expecting a baby." There was a long pause.

"A baby? Are you sure?" Alex sounded stunned.

"Yes, I'm sure," Alex was making Red nervous. "Alex, I'm just as surprised as you are. But we need to know how we're going to work this out."

"Okay, Red, can I call you back? I'm in the middle of something."

"Sure, I'll wait up for you," Red said and hung up.

Red didn't hear back from Alex that night or the next day or the day after that. She called him several times and left messages, but he never returned any of her calls. She remembered from one of their long conversations that he had mentioned one of his best friends by the name of Paul Dumar. She was able to locate a number for Paul and reached out to him. He told Red that Alex had told him about their relationship but that he had not spoken with him in a couple of weeks. Red asked Paul to call Alex and have him contact her. When she didn't hear back from Paul after a few days, she called him again and it rang into his voice mail. She hung up without leaving a message, because somehow she knew he would not return her call. She tried a few more times to reach Alex, and the last time she called him, the number was no longer in service.

Red was gaining weight rapidly and started to get concerned. She had never had a child, so she did not have a barometer to go by. On her next doctor's visit, she voiced her concern. The doctor said not to worry, but she would schedule an ultrasound to make sure everything was okay. By this time, she was already five months along. When the results of the ultrasound came back, Red was hit with another bombshell. The ultrasound showed that she was having twins — a girl and a boy. She had already been contemplating how her life was going to change raising a child. She was secure enough in her job and the agency had assured her that she had nothing to worry about as far as continuing with them after she had the baby. But now the plot had thickened; she was having twins.

Red knew within herself that she was not cut out to be a mother, and two children was completely out of the question. Moreover, Alex had dropped off the face of the Earth and she was terrified at the thought of raising children. She wanted to consider adoption, but then she wasn't comfortable with the idea of a total stranger raising her babies. All at once, she had an idea. She knew that James and Pamela had been trying to conceive for the last three years, without success. They so desperately wanted children.

The next evening Red called her sister Pam and told her that she needed to come visit over the weekend. She said that it was an important matter that couldn't be discussed over the phone. Pam said sure, no problem.

When she hung up the phone, Pam said to James, "Red wants to stop by this weekend. She said she needs to discuss something important with us. I wonder what it could be."

"Knowing your sister," James laughed, "It could be anything. I wouldn't even try to guess."

Red arrived on Sunday afternoon, only this time there was no fanfare, no grand entrance. She quietly came through the door, and when she did, Pam almost fainted. He sister was obviously expecting a child. Pam stared at her in disbelief. She would never have guessed in a million years that flighty, flirty Red would be expecting. She was the one who had vowed never to be tied down with a husband or children. But what she said next was even more unbelievable.

She looked at Pam and James with tears in her eyes and said, "I have to something to ask both of you. I hope that your answer will be yes, because if not, I'm not sure what I will do." With tears now flowing freely, she proceeded to recount the events that occurred over the past several months. When she finished, she said "I'm having twins, but I don't want to keep the babies. I want to ask you and James if you could take them and raise them. I just can't do it alone."

## CHAPTER EIGHT

Pamela sat down at her desk and began writing. She felt so lonely and so old. It had been almost one year since she had been confined to a wheelchair and even though James took excellent care of her without ever complaining, she still couldn't help but feel that she was a burden. All of the unbelief and devastation from the last twelve months since the accident seemed to be closing in on her. She was sick of the doctor's visits and the medications and the therapy sessions. The only ray of sunshine had been the wonderful physical therapist that she had finally ended up with. She had been a Godsend. Pamela had formed a bond with her and had never seen anyone with so much patience. She was truly a gift.

Although she had accepted and fully knew that she would never walk again, still some days she felt as though she was stuck in a horrific dream and thought that she would wake up and be back in her office at the firm. There would be fresh flowers on her desk and client files that she had to comb through. There would be meetings and conference calls and interaction with her colleagues.

There would be lunches with co-workers and late dinners with clients. There would be her perfect life with James and the twins, complete with all the laughter and love that always filled her home. No matter how tired she was after working long hours, she would always somehow seem to get a second wind and a burst of energy when she arrived home. She had loved her life and her accomplishments. She had always felt extremely blessed and she never took it for granted. She was thankful each and every day for her family, friends and her job.

Shortly after the accident, the partners at the firm had come to her home and met with her to decide how to delegate her workload to some of the junior attorneys. She had blatantly opposed this idea, stating that there was no way that they could do an effective of a job as she could. She had camaraderie with all of her clients and made herself available to them 24/7. She was one of the hardest working attorneys at the firm, even given her status as senior partner. She still personally went over each client file that was assigned to her. She had a top-notch personal assistant, but she still liked to involve herself in every aspect of each case.

The partners had finally gotten her to agree to lighten her workload by about 40%. But there was only so much she could do working from home. She was still able to participate in some conference calls and the quarterly firm meetings by teleconference. But after a while, she noticed that the partners had started to not include her in some meetings. Once, when she questioned them about why she was not informed of a teleconference, they replied that they had scheduled it at the last minute, and did not want to bother her, and that the junior associates were stepping up and doing an excellent job.

About three weeks after that, the partners approached her with the idea of her working in an "Of Counsel" capacity, which meant she was not required to be in the office at all, and her case load would be streamlined even more.

Pam remembered a television show from years ago called "The Invisible Man." He could be standing right in a room and no one could see him. He could switch lights off and on, knock things over and just run rampant without anyone being able to stop him.

She had to laugh in spite of herself as she found herself thinking, "I wish I could be invisible and just go to the office and disrupt meetings, interrupt phone conferences, scatter papers everywhere and generally make things miserable for everyone."

She laughed again and didn't realize how loud she was laughing until James came into the room and said, "What's so funny in here?"

"Oh nothing," she replied while still chuckling to herself.

"Well, whatever it was, I'm glad to see you smiling. You've been having a rough time of it. But you know I'm here for you. We're in this together."

She looked at James and smiled. Things had eventually gotten better between them. She shuddered when she remembered what a monster she had been the first few weeks and months following the accident. She had apologized to her family for some of the terrible things she had said to them. Angie and Aaron had told her they understood and were just glad that things were getting back to at least some state of normalcy.

Aaron, ever the jokester, said he had nicknamed her "Broom-Hilda," after a cartoon character witch.

James was such a jewel. If anyone could be perfect, it would be him. He had always been a wonderful husband and provider. To know James Burke was to love him. She knew that some of her friends envied her life. A wonderful husband, two great children, and a stellar career. Who could ask for more? God had certainly been good to her. Even though things were not as she wanted, it was still a blessing to be alive and surrounded by such a wonderful family.

"Well, I'll be in the den if you need anything," James said as he left the room.

"Thanks, Honey, I'm fine. I'm just going to do some writing." Apparently, James didn't hear her mention writing, because if he had, he would have probably thought that was peculiar. She had no pressing cases, and she normally did more reading than anything else. She left the correspondence and compiling of legal briefs to her assistant. And right now, with only a small number of cases to work on, she had very little reading to do.

She was thankful that he had not heard her and asked any questions. Now was the time. She knew it had to be done, but she had procrastinated because it was going to be painful. But it was now or never. She opened her laptop, closed her eyes for a few seconds and took a deep breath, and began to write.

Angie and Aaron came through the back door that led into the kitchen. They could tell that their mom had been in the kitchen because the dishwasher was on the rinse cycle. Pamela was able to do quite a few things independently. She used a motorized wheelchair, and James had had the kitchen remodeled right after the accident so that the appliances were at a height that would be accessible to her. The bathroom in the master bedroom had also been restructured so that she could roll her wheelchair in and transfer to a shower seat.

Still a bottomless pit, Aaron went straight to the refrigerator. "Hmmm…not much here," he chuckled. He always joked that there was nothing there to eat, but then proceeded to make a mile-high plate of sandwiches, chips, fruit and usually some kind of dessert. Along with that he would down a large glass of milk or juice.

Angie looked at him and shook her head. "Not fair. Not fair at all. If I ate like that, I wouldn't fit through the door."

"Sorry, kiddo," Aaron thumped Angie lightly on the head. "That's the breaks, I guess. Can't help you." Angie loved her twin brother, and no matter how much he teased her, she never got truly upset with him. But she really did wish she could eat like that, at least occasionally.

"Ah, what's this?" Aaron noticed an envelope on the table that said "Angie and Aaron" on the front.

"A mystery letter addressed to both of us. I'll open it, I'm the oldest."

"Feel free," Angie said and laughed. "If it's a letter bomb, then it will get you first."

Aaron shot her a glance. "That was mean of you to say."

"Well, you want to take the lead, let's see how you look with missing fingers." Angie poked her tongue out at Aaron.

As he looked closer, he said "Angie, this is Mom's handwriting."

"What? Angie's laughter quickly turned to concern. She looked toward her parents' bedroom, which was just down the hall from the kitchen. The door was closed, and they knew that their mom was usually reading or watching television when they got home in the afternoon. She looked back at Aaron and could instinctively sense that they were both thinking the same thing — that whatever they were about to read was not going to be good news.

Aaron slowly opened the envelope. Angie sat close to him and they both began to read the letter.

*Dear Aaron and Angela,*

*I don't know where to begin. I don't know how you both will feel after reading this. You've both heard of how your father and I met. We were childhood sweethearts, attended high school and college together, and were married shortly after graduating from law school. We both started our careers as attorneys at the same time. We were blissfully in love and couldn't be happier. Of course we wanted to start a family, and talked about having two children. It was our wish that we would have a girl and a boy to complete our little circle. After about three years of trying without success, we decided to visit a doctor to see if there was a medical reason as to why I could not conceive. As it turned out, I had a condition called "endometriosis," which is an infection of the lining of the uterus, and it rendered me infertile. As you can imagine, we were crushed. We thought about adopting, but then decided against that. So we finally resigned ourselves to the fact that there would be no children for us. I still prayed to God for a miracle because I wanted more than anything to be a mother. The following year, my prayers were answered when Red called me late one night and said that she needed to talk to your father and me. She came to visit that weekend and told your father and me that she was expecting twins, and wanted to know if we would take the responsibility to raise them as our own. Your biological father was no longer in her life, and she could not do it alone. We gladly accepted, and, as the cliché goes, the rest is history.*

*We wanted to tell you, but she swore us to secrecy. But now I feel this is the time you should know. When the plane was going down, I promised myself that if God spared my life, I would let you know the truth. My whole life flashed in front of my eyes, and I remembered the first day I laid eyes on you and instantly fell in love. I remembered all the birthday parties when Red came and showered you with gifts. I wanted so badly to tell you that she was your mother and a few times I almost did, but I had made a vow to keep the secret. It pained me to see how she looked at you, knowing that she was your mother but not being able to share that with you.*

*Christmas was always the hardest for her and for your father and me as well. But yet we went on living the lie. The difficult part about that is that when you tell one lie, you have to tell another one to prop up the last one. It became extremely exhausting, but worse than that, we became very good at it. And that was the disturbing part.*

*Your father does not know I'm writing this letter. I hope you can both forgive us for keeping this from you for so long, but I have had a lot of days and nights to think about things since my injury. I cannot hold this secret any longer. I love you both so very much.*

*Love, Mom*


Angie's head was spinning. She could not believe what she had just read. Aaron was staring at the letter in disbelief. They were both still sitting at the table trying to digest what had just happened when their father walked in from the den where he had been going through some papers.

"Why do you two look as if you've just seen a ghost?" he

looked from Aaron to Angie, whose faces were both as white as a sheet. "What's going on here?" their father asked again.

Not being able to speak, they both just stared at their father. He saw the tears in their eyes. "Is Mom okay?" he started to rush toward the bedroom.

"Dad, Mom is all right," Aaron spoke up. "Dad please sit down. We need to show you something."

When James finished reading the letter, his face was ashen. He wished that Pamela would have told him that she had decided to tell the twins. If only he would have known, he could possibly have prevented her from writing the letter. He regretted the day that they had promised Red that they would never disclose the truth. Of course, they both knew it was the wrong thing to do, but they had wanted children so badly that they went along with Red's terms. But he had always feared that this day would come and somehow the twins would find out who their birth mother was. Their family was small, and there was no one outside of the family and the adoption attorney who knew the truth. And, of course, both Pamela and James had informed their employers that they were adopting.

Red was very seldom present. Still a world traveler, she visited on their birthday and Christmas. That was it. Now here he was, sitting across from Angie and Aaron who both seemed to be looking at him with disgust in their eyes. He didn't know what to say to them in this moment.

Angie's mind now went back to when they were growing up and Aunt Red always flew in each year for their birthday party from wherever she happened to be at the time. She would shower them with lavish gifts. Friends sometimes remarked that Angie resembled Red more than she did her own mother. Pamela would reply, "Yes, Red had them spoiled from day one, so I guess that's why Angie looks so much like her." To which everyone would laugh and say, "That's what Aunties are for!"

Now it was all making sense. Red would also come for Christmas and again show up with a roomful of gifts and toys and clothes for them. Now Angie was starting to remember the way Red always looked at her and Aaron. Something was different about it; a few times she thought she saw tears in Red's eyes. Now she was sure she did. She would always hug them so tightly and for such a long time when she was leaving. She would tell them, "You are the best niece and nephew anyone could ever have. I love you to the moon and back."

Aaron stared at the floor. He was also remembering growing up seeing Aunt Red on their birthday and at Christmas. She would always ruffle his hair and say, "You're a good looking young man, you know that?" She would always tell them that if there was ever anything they wanted or needed, to have their parents contact her. Of course, none of this seemed strange at the time. After all she only had one niece and nephew. Now he knew, she had no nieces or nephews, but two children.

The reality of it started to set in and he was no longer able to hold back the tears. "Dad," he said between sobs, "How could you and mom do this? What was so hard about telling us the truth? Thank God our birth mother is a family member, but that still doesn't make it any easier knowing that you and Mom waited so long to tell us. And it took a major tragedy for that to even happen."

Now Angie knew why they had never seen pictures of their mother when she was pregnant. Once when they were viewing family albums, she and Aaron had asked if there were any pictures of her while she was carrying them, and she replied "No, I was so huge and didn't like to take any pictures."

It went right over Aaron's head, but Angie thought it a bit strange because she thought women liked to have pictures to look back on.  It was such a fun and enjoyable time. She wasn't quite old enough then to understand, but at least that's what she thought. The only pictures they were shown were when their mom and dad were holding them as babies and then all the other pictures as they were growing up. And yes, Aunt Red always took tons of pictures with them, and now in hindsight, there was that look in her eyes when she looked at them. It even showed through the pictures. A real mother's love cannot be disguised, no matter what.

Angie got up from the table and was about to head in the direction of her mom's bedroom, but just as she did, Pamela opened the door and came out. She joined them in the kitchen. She looked from Aaron to Angie and then at James. He looked like a lost child. She felt that she had betrayed him by letting the truth out, but at the same time she hoped he understood that it had to be done.

Angie was the first to speak. "Mom, how could you and Dad do this to us?" Angie burst into tears. She hadn't wanted to cry. She had wanted to scream at her mom and dad and tell them they were cowards. She wanted to tell them that she would never forgive them for what they had done. She wanted to bang her fists on the table and tell them that they had no right to hold the truth from them. She felt as if her identity had been taken away from her. Her whole life up until now was a farce. And not only her, but Aaron as well.

As if she was reading Angie's mind, Pamela began to speak. "Angie, I want you and Aaron to understand that it was not an easy decision. We loved you from the day Red told us that she was expecting. And when she said it was twins, we felt as if God had answered our prayers. I know you feel like screaming right now, and you would be totally in your rights to do so. I know you want to hate us, and I would not blame you for that either. Maybe it seems that we took the cowards' way out, but we did it out of love for you. I can't tell you how many nights your dad and I lay in bed and contemplated telling you the truth. But we had promised Red, and so we talked ourselves out of it. We should have told you years ago and let the chips fall where they may."

## CHAPTER NINE

Angie went to her room and called Kenny. She literally needed a shoulder to cry on right now, and he was the closest person to her other than her immediate family. As soon as he heard Angie's voice, Kenny could tell something was wrong. He knew her so well. "Angie, what is it?" Kenny could hear the nervousness in her voice.

"Can you come over? I need to talk to you." Angie's voice was cracking. Without missing a beat, Kenny replied, "I'll be right there."

Kenny read the letter in disbelief. When he finished, he hugged Angie tightly for a long moment. "I am so shocked," he finally managed to say.

"Not as shocked as we were," Angie still couldn't believe it. "Can you imagine finding out the people who raised you are not your biological parents? I feel like I have been sucker punched."

"How is Aaron taking it?" Kenny asked.

"Well, you know Aaron. He hides his feelings well, but I know he is really hurt."

"Yeah, I'll go in and talk to him before I leave," Kenny said.

"Kenny, I really appreciate you coming over."

"No problem, at all." Kenny smiled. She looked so sad. He hated to see her like this. "I know this has to be devastating for you. I wish there was something more I could do."

Angie thought about asking him how Julie was doing, just out of politeness, but truthfully, she didn't care. "You've done enough just by being here. I didn't know who else to call." Angie was so glad he had come right over. Even though their relationship had changed, he would always be a dear friend. They had history together and that was something that would never change. They had parted as friends, and she knew she could always depend on him, and vice-versa.

"Angie," Kenny chose his words carefully, "Can I ask you something?"

"Sure, anything." Angie wondered where this was going.

"Well," Kenny looked her in the eyes, "I've been thinking a lot about us, and I don't know how to say this, but I'll just say it. I made a mistake by breaking up with you. Yes, I was attracted to Julie when I first met her. But as we started spending more time together, there were so many little things that I didn't like about her. Bottom line up top, she just wasn't you."

Angie was looking at Kenny intently. Was Kenny really saying what she thought he was? Or was this all a crazy dream that she would wake up from at any minute? Maybe the letter had been part of the dream as well. She was sure that she was in "The Twilight Zone." A smile crossed her face as she thought to herself, "I really do watch too much television."

Kenny continued, "Angie, I'm so sorry about all this, and I'm sorry that I've added to your pain. Can we try to pick up where we left off?" Angie was not sure what to say. Kenny looked worried. "If you need some time to think about it, I totally understand. But at least say you will think about it."

Angie look at Kenny. She knew him well enough to know that he was truly sorry for what had happened and that he honestly wanted to rekindle their relationship. She smiled at Kenny. "Okay, we can pick up where we left off. I would like that. But right now I need to call Red."

Kenny squeezed her hand. "Do it."

Angie's hands were shaking as she dialed Red's number. She still could not believe what had transpired. She and Aaron had decided that they needed to talk to Red face to face. Now it felt strange calling her "Aunt Red" knowing that she was their real mother. As if the near-death incident had not been enough, they were now given the devastating news that the two individuals whom they had known as their mother and father for their entire lives were in fact their aunt and uncle. It was like something out of a movie.

"Hello Niecy!" Red answered cheerily. How are you doing sweetie?"

"Hey Aunt Red, I'm fine. Aaron and I need to talk to you."

"Sure," replied Red. "Is he on the line with you?"

"No he's not." Angie tried to keep her voice steady. "We need to talk in person. We were wondering if you could arrange a quick trip home."

"Angie, what's wrong? Is something going on with Pam?"

Angie could the hear the panic in Red's voice "No, no, everyone is fine. We just need to discuss something with you."

"Okay, I can be there the day after tomorrow," Red answered.

"Ok, thanks and see you then." Angie hung up the phone. Now she and Aaron just had to prepare themselves for meeting with Red. For the first time, Aaron did not have a joke or funny comment. This was definitely not a laughing matter.

Red arrived early on Saturday morning. There was a look of concern on her face. James and Pam and the twins were all in the kitchen just finishing breakfast. It had been very awkward for the past couple of days following the letter. You could still cut the tension in the air with a knife. Angie and Aaron had hardly spoken more than a few words to their parents. It was still a lot to digest.

Red poured herself a cup of coffee and joined the family at the table. She looked over at her sister who had a strained look on her face. She saw that James was just looking down at the floor. "Okay, who wants to tell me exactly what is going on here? The suspense is killing me."

Angie and Aaron looked at each other and finally Aaron said, "I'll start."

"Aunt Red, our mom gave Angie and me some shocking news the other night. She wrote us a letter, and in the letter she informed us of the true facts concerning our birth." Red's face dropped. She looked over at Pam who could not even make eye contact with her. The blood started to drain from Red's face as she knew what was coming next. Aaron proceeded to tell her everything that was written in the letter. When he finished speaking, the room was so silent that you could hear a feather drop on the carpet.

Angie spoke up, "Aunt Red, we can almost understand why you made the choice not to keep us, but why did you want to keep it a secret? Did you never want to be identified with us at all as our mother? Or did you just want to pose as this doting and adoring aunt who showed up on our birthday and Christmas? What was so difficult about just telling us the truth from the beginning?"

Red swallowed hard and began to speak through tears. "When I learned that I was going to be a mother, I was happy, even though it was unplanned. But then when your father ghosted me, I was disappointed, hurt and felt like a failure. I felt like no one deserved to have me as a mother. I felt that I had made a mistake, and that you deserved a better life, one with a mother *and* a father. I knew James and Pam wanted children and I knew they would make the perfect parents. That is why I made them promise to never tell you who I was and to just let you see me as your aunt who loved and adored you. I never meant to hurt you. I hope you can understand and forgive me."

Angie stared at Red for a long moment. "I understand, I really do, but it is going to take some time for me to forgive you.

All of you." She looked at James and Pamela.

Aaron spoke directly to Red. "I can't say that I fully understand and, if I'm being honest, it will take me some time to forgive you."

Red looked from Angie to Aaron. "Thank you both," she spoke in a whisper. Then to James and Pam she said, "I'm so sorry that I asked you to keep this secret for all these years. It took a tragedy for the truth to come out. I'm sorry for the pain I have caused everyone. I know it will be a long, slow process, but I hope that we can all grow from here and put this behind us."

Angie and Aaron got up and walked over to Red and hugged her as they all broke down in tears. Then one by one, they went to James and Pam and hugged them as well. No words were needed. It was going to be a long, slow process, but the healing had begun.

# *EPILOGUE*

## James and Pamela — Purple and Blue

James and Pamela finally found themselves empty nesters after both Angie and Aaron went away to college. James continues his work as an attorney advocating for father's rights. Pamela is an adjunct professor and teaches law at her alma mater, St. Mary's University School of Law. She drives a specially equipped vehicle that uses long handles to operate the gas and brake pedals. She is almost totally independent in spite of her disability. She is often called upon to speak at functions for people who have suffered debilitating injuries to let them know that it's not the end just because you suffer a tragic event. If you lived through it, then there's more to be done. She is a living testament that what doesn't kill you makes you stronger.

## Aaron — Green

Aaron decided to concentrate on the two-legged variety as opposed to becoming a veterinarian, and obtained a Medical Degree in the field of Internal Medicine. But he still has a love for pets. He and his two dogs, Steven and Suzy Q, and three cats, Maria, Lilly and Elizabeth, live just outside of San

Antonio. No wife or children as of yet.

## Angie — Pink

Angie and Kenny are married and have two children — twin boys. Yes, multiples absolutely run in families. They often reminisce about how they met in high school and still laugh about the "Julie" chapter. Angie jokingly tells Kenny that she had contemplated putting a hit out on Julie. Julie later went away to school and Kenny lost touch with her. Kenny's mom, Debra, met a wonderful man and remarried and moved to a small town near

Kansas. She still continues to work with battered women.

## Regina — Red

Ahhh Red, we can't say enough about Red. The protagonist. Love her or hate her — there's no in between. But she really does have a heart of gold.

Out of love she created a situation that almost cost her dearly. But in the end when all was said and done, all of the colors congealed.

Red is now the CEO of her own modeling agency. She coaches aspiring models and still travels extensively scouting and teaching classes. Aaron refers to her as

"Auntie-Mommy." Angie still calls her "Aunt Red."

The entire family still gathers at the home of James and Pamela Burke every Christmas.

\*\*\*\*\*\*\*\*\*\*

If you enjoyed COLORS, more to come…

Talk to me via email at: sylvia.carlton@ymail.com

or find me on social media:

Facebook: @sylviacarlton

Instagram: @sylvia.carlton.1

Twitter: @carltonsylvia